First U.S. edition 2002

Library of Congress Cataloging-in-Publication Data

Murphy, Jill.
All for one / Jill Murphy. —1st U.S. ed.
p. cm.
Summary: Marlon tries very hard to be part of the neighborhood games until he finds something else to do that makes everyone want to join him.
ISBN 0-7636-0785-1
[1. Play—Fiction. 2. Friendship—Fiction. 3. Monsters—Fiction.] I. Title.
PZ7.M9534 Ai 1999 [E]—dc21 98-029218

2 4 6 8 10 9 7 5 3 1

Printed in China

This book was typeset in Stone Informal.
The illustrations were done in pen and colored pencil.

Candlewick Press
2067 Massachusetts Avenue
Cambridge, Massachusetts 02140

visit us at www.candlewick.com

ALL FOR ONE

CANDLEWICK PRESS
CAMBRIDGE, MASSACHUSETTS

Marlon had run out of things to do. He had done lots of drawing,

and built a secret cave out of the sofa cushions.

He had made a big castle
out of the videos, blown
it up with his special
alien powers . . .

and helped his army on a dangerous mission up the bookcase.

"I wish I had someone to play with," said Marlon. "I can't think of anything else to do."

"Well," said Marlon's granny, "you can tidy up this room for a start. It looks as if a bomb hit it."

"A bomb *did* hit it," said Marlon. "My alien space

bomb blew everything up."

"Don't be ridiculous," said Marlon's mom. "Come on, I'll help you tidy up. Then you can see who's out playing—there might be a game you could join. I'll fix the cushions."

"Okay," said Marlon. "I'll fix the videos."

Marlon went outside and found Basher, Boomps-a-Daisy, and Alligatina all bashing each other with swords.

"What are you playing?" asked Marlon.

"The Three Musketeers," said Boomps-a-Daisy.

"Can *I* play?" asked Marlon.

"No," said Basher. "There's only *three* musketeers. Can't you count? There aren't *four*."

"Yes, there are," said Marlon. "There's four when that other one joins later. I could be the other one, and their motto *is* All for One —"

"And One for All except Marlon!" sneered Alligatina.

"Can't I play anyway?" pleaded Marlon.

"We'll think about it," said Basher.

Marlon rushed home.
"I just *have* to be a musketeer, Mom!" he said.
"If I get dressed up, they might let me play!"

Marlon put on a big T-shirt and his mom made him a cloak out of an old curtain. His granny lent him a hat she had worn to a wedding. Marlon put his best sword into his belt and pulled on his boots.

"Perfect!" said his mom.

Marlon ran back to the others.
"Here I am!" he said.

"We aren't musketeers anymore," explained Boomps-a-Daisy. "We're pirates now."

"I can see that," said Marlon.

"He could be the cabin boy," said Alligatina.

"Could I?" said Marlon. "Pleeeease."

"We'll think about it," said Basher.

Marlon rushed back home.
"I have to be a pirate now!"
he shouted. "Quick!"

Marlon's mom found a scarf and sewed some curtain rings onto it. She made him an eye patch, and Marlon put on his striped T-shirt with a cutlass in his belt.
"Great!" said his mom.

Marlon raced back to the others.
"Here I am!" he said.

But the others weren't pirates anymore. They were doing handstands and swinging on the jungle gym.

"What are you doing now?" asked Marlon.

"We're having a gymnastic contest," said Basher. "We're not playing pirates anymore."

Marlon gave up. He wasn't very good at gymnastic contests, especially ones with Basher in them.

“What’s the matter, dear?” asked Marlon’s mom
as he slouched into the kitchen.
“They keep changing the game,” said Marlon—
“Can we fill up the new wading pool?”
“It’s a little chilly outside,” said Marlon’s mom.
“We could fill it with warm water,” said Marlon—
“Pleeeeeeeease?”

"He'll catch a cold," warned Granny. "He'll freeze to death in a wading pool in this weather."

Marlon's mom looked at Marlon, all dressed up in his pirate outfit and no one to play with.

"All right, then," she said. "Go and get your swimming things."

"You spoil that little monster," muttered Marlon's granny.

While Marlon changed into his swimming things,
his mom connected the garden hose to the kitchen faucet
and filled the pool until it began to steam in the cold air.

Marlon's granny watched from the window. "This is ridiculous," she said. "In my day we just sat quietly and read a book."

Marlon leapt in.
"I'm a famous underwater explorer," he said.
"I'm hunting the rare and extremely dangerous giant pink starfish!"

Marlon's granny brought him a drink and a piece of cake. "We don't want him starving as well as freezing," she said.

Then it began to rain, so Marlon's mom fixed up an umbrella to keep the cake from getting soggy.

On their way home, Alligatina, Boomps-a-Daisy, and Basher looked over the wall.

"What a cool pool," said Alligatina. "It's really big."

"We could all get in there with you," said Boomps-a-Daisy.

“What are you playing?” asked Basher.
“Underwater explorers,” said Marlon.
“I wish we’d thought of that,” said Basher.
“Can we come and play tomorrow?”

Marlon leaned back and took a sip of orange juice.

"I'll think about it," he said.